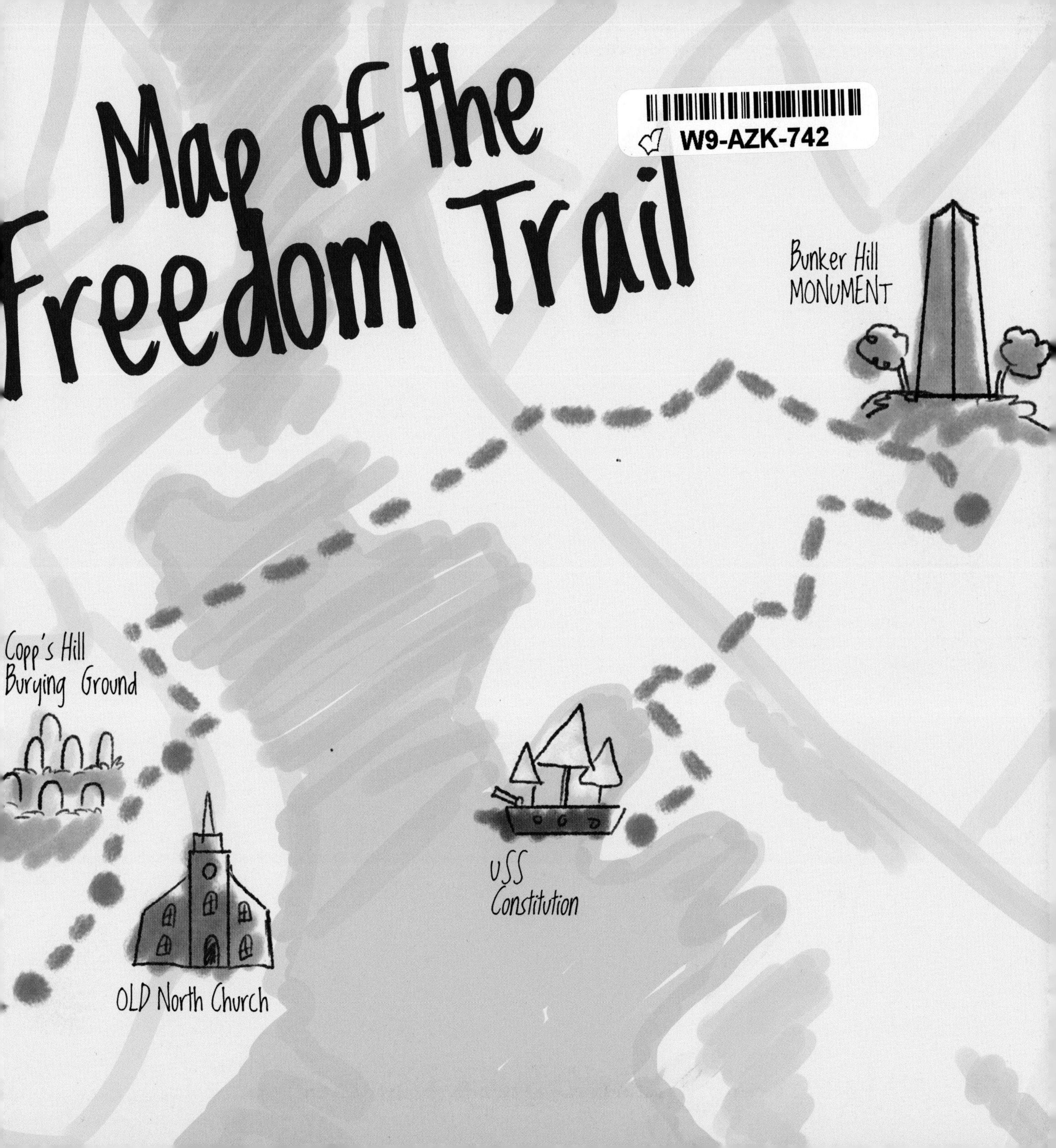

Map of the Freedom Trail

Little Mouse's
on the Freedom Trail
Written by Brittany Bang
Illustrations by Caitlyn Knepka
BOSTON

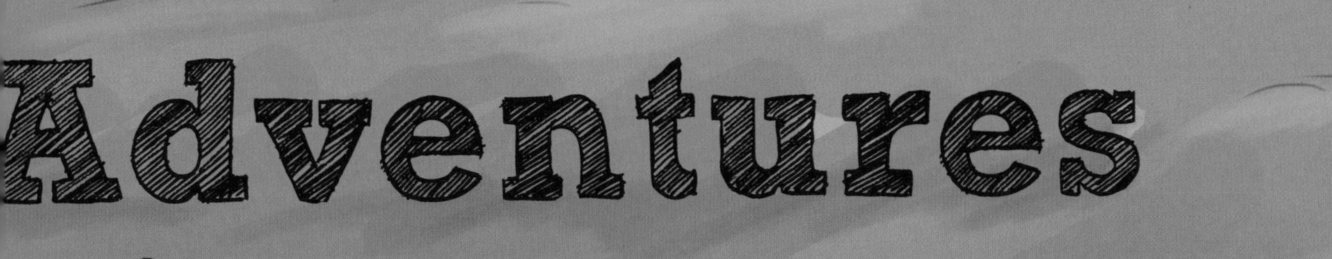

CURLY Q PRESS

This book is dedicated to my mom. Thank you for being the best Ya Ya in the world to my little boy, Jackson, and for taking him on so many adventures around Boston.

Written by Brittany Bang
Illustrations by Caitlyn Knepka

www.littlemousesadventures.com

Published by CurlyQ Press
Mansfield, Massachusetts
www.CurlyQPress.com

Library of Congress Control Number:
2014957998
ISBN: 978-1-941216-06-4
E-ISBN: 978-1-941216-07-1
Printed in the United States of America

For more information about the Freedom Trail visit:
thefreedomtrail.org

As Little Mouse rolls over she can feel a warm beam of sunlight on her whiskers. She opens one eye and peers out her window to see a big blue sky.

“Oh, my, what a beautiful day in Boston!” she squeaks. “Today will be the perfect day to visit many of my favorite places around the city.”

"But, Little Mouse, Boston is very big, with so much to see, how will you not get lost along the way?"

"Oh, that's easy! All I do is follow the red line."

And with that, Little Mouse throws on her backpack and runs down the steps of Fenway Park.

"The red line? What red line, Little Mouse?"

"The red line that starts in my favorite park, Boston Common. This line shows me, and all our visitors, where some of the most historic places are in the city."

Little Mouse scampers down the beautiful streets of Boston, past shops and restaurants...

...and on through the Public Garden, where she passes by the famous Swan Boats but does not stop to smell the flowers!

"That sounds very exciting, Little Mouse! Can I come?"

"Yes, you can join me on my adventure on the FREEDOM TRAIL! The Freedom Trail is Boston's famous two-and-a-half mile path linking sixteen sites of the American Revolution together, making it easy to see and learn about this very important part of early American history. The Trail was first formed in 1951, and the red line was added in 1958 to help guide visitors."

"Our next stop on the Trail is the Massachusetts State House. It was built in 1798 and is one of the most recognizable buildings in Boston because of its beautiful gold dome. It was originally made of wood and first covered in copper by Paul Revere, and later covered in gold in 1874."

"What happens at the State House, Little Mouse?"

"Oh, this is where our senators, state representatives, and the governor conduct the business of Massachusetts. It is a very important place!"

Little Mouse continues down the street and passes by Park Street Church.

"Visitors recognize this church because of its 217-foot-high steeple, which rises high into the sky."

Little Mouse skips along the Freedom Trail, and while winding through the cobblestone streets of Boston, she passes by the...

KING'S CHAPEL BURYING GROUND
Chilton
Winthrop
BENJAMIN FRANKLIN STATUE
BOSTON LATIN SCHOOL SITE

"Oh, this is one of my favorite buildings in all of Boston!" exclaims Little Mouse. "This is the Old Corner Bookstore, and I love reading books! Built in 1718, it was one of the most important buildings in book publishing, and many famous authors have visited here over the years."

"What is this big brick building, Little Mouse?"

"This is the Old South Meeting House. It was built in 1729, and some of the most important meetings about the American Revolution took place here. One of those meetings discussed the planning of the Boston Tea Party. This was when a group of men, called the Sons of Liberty, did not want to pay taxes on the tea that came from England. So, late one night, they snuck onto the ships carrying the tea and dumped it all into the harbor!"

Little Mouse soon finds herself looking at a brick building surrounded by skyscrapers.

"This is the Old State House—one of the most famous buildings in Boston. This is where the Declaration of Independence was first read in Boston on July 18, 1776. The Declaration of Independence stated that the thirteen American colonies now wanted to be a new nation and no longer part of Great Britain. This new nation was called the United States of America."

"Little Mouse, what is happening in front of the Old State House? What is everyone doing?"

"Oh, that is the spot where the Boston Massacre took place on March 5, 1770. It was a battle between the British redcoats and the colonists living in Boston. The colonists were angry about the British soldiers possibly taking over in the town, which led to this fight. This was one of the many incidents that started the Revolutionary War. Every year, Bostonians reenact the Boston Massacre to teach visitors about this very important event in history."

"Hurray! We have made it to Faneuil Hall. This building was built in 1741, by Peter Faneuil, as a place to trade and sell goods. But, it was also a place where lots of people would gather for town meetings."

"Today Faneuil Hall, and the surrounding buildings called Quincy Market and Faneuil Hall Marketplace, are a favorite place to meet and visit friends, because of all the wonderful shops and food!"

Even after a rest, and a full belly, Little Mouse's paws are getting very tired.

"The Freedom Trail is quite the journey for a small mouse. I am glad my friend Audrey, the bulldog, is here to help me make it to the end!"

"We're not at the end yet, Little Mouse?"

"Oh, no, there are still many wonderful sites left to see! Besides, my favorite stop along the whole Trail is at the very end. We must keep going!"

ittle Mouse, Audrey, and riends continue on their dventure, passing by three ore important historic sites.

OLD NORTH CHURCH

This is the oldest standing church building in Boston (built in 1723).

The lantern signals that started the American Revolution, which inspired the saying "One if by land two if by sea," were sent from this church.

COPP'S HILL BURYING GROUND

PAUL REVERE HOUSE

This is downtown Boston's oldest building (built circa 1680) and was owned by the American patriot Paul Revere from 1770 to 1800.

On the eve of April 18, 1775, Paul Revere left from this house to warn fellow patriots that the British were coming. This would later be known as the "Midnight Ride of Paul Revere."

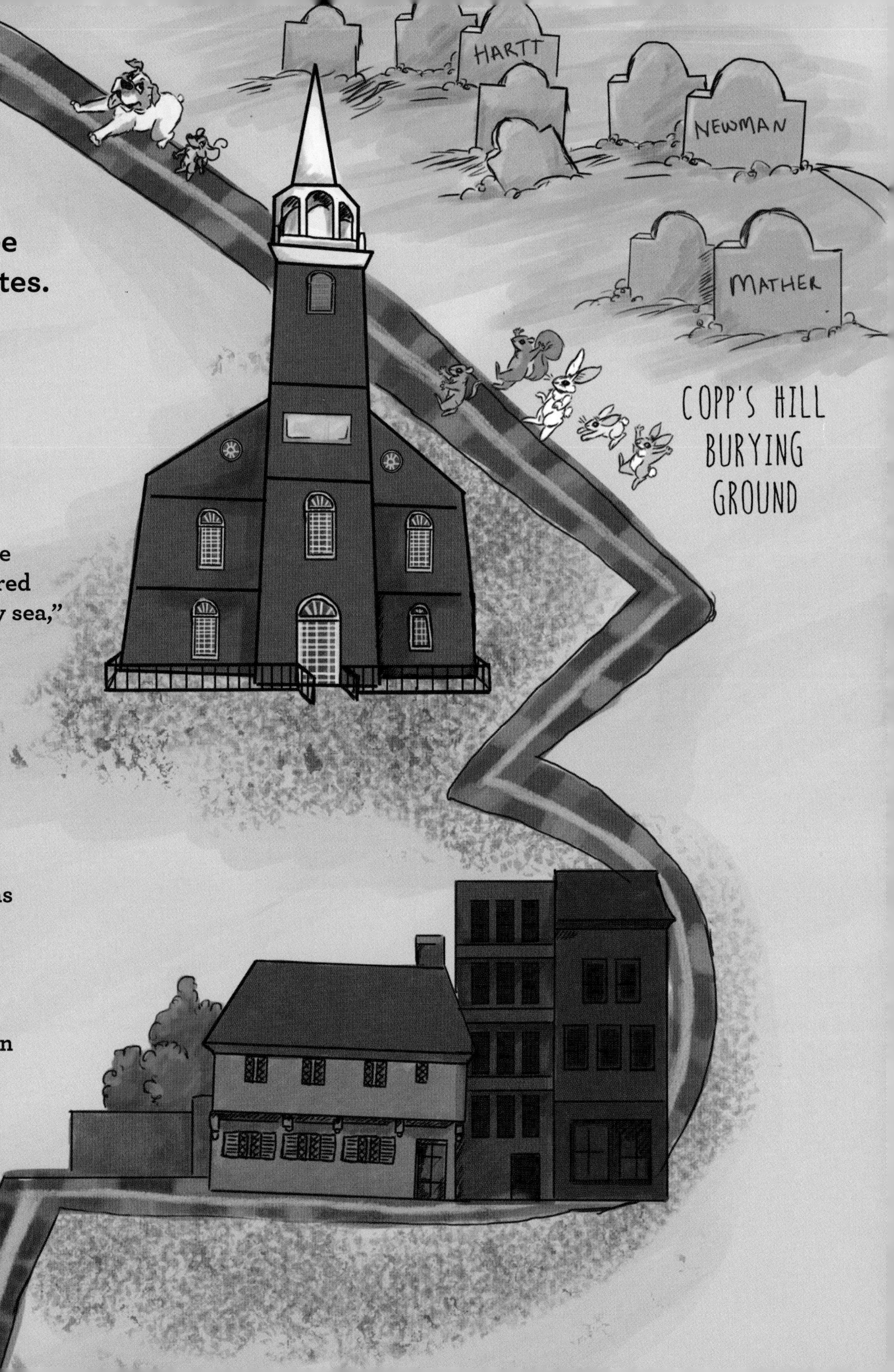

"Little Mouse, what is that big white tower up ahead?"

"That is the Bunker Hill Monument, which shows where the Battle of Bunker Hill took place on June 17, 1775. They started building it fifty years after the battle, in 1825, and it took almost seventeen years to complete! This was the first major battle of the Revolutionary War."

As Little Mouse rounds the corner, her eyes get big and wide and she squeals in delight.

"We're here! We made it! We made it to the end of the Trail! We have followed the red line all throughout Boston, visited fifteen historic sites, and have made it to the sixteenth and final stop—the *USS Constitution!"*

Little mouse scampers off to board the United States Navy warship located in the Charlestown Navy Yard.

“I think this is the most beautiful ship in the world! Built in 1797, she is most famous for sailing in the War of 1812. She was so well built, it seemed like cannonballs bounced right off her, giving her the nickname “Old Ironsides.”

“Today, the *USS Constitution* sails into Boston Harbor only a few times a year, most famously on July 4th, to celebrate Independence Day.”

Well, the sun begins to set and Little Mouse makes her way back to her nest inside the walls of Fenway Park.

"What a wonderful day we had, Little Mouse! We walked the Freedom Trail, learned about the history of Boston, and even went on a big ship. When can we do all of these wonderful things again?"

NEY REFUNDS
NDSTAND
ROW
SEAT
3
15
SEPT. 28
1966
CITGO
MATCH
250 MATCHES
OF · KITCHEN MATCHES · CLOSE BOX BEFORE STRIKING

"Anytime you wish, silly. Boston, and all of its wonderful sights can be visited all year long, and each time you visit you will learn something new."

And with that, Little Mouse drifts off to sleep dreaming about her next big adventure.

BOSTON COMMON
MASSACHUSETTS STATE HOUSE
Granary Burying Ground
King's Chapel & King's Chapel Burying Ground
Park STREET Church
Boston Latin School Site
Benjamin Franklin Statue
FANEUIL HAL
OLD South Meeting HOUSE
OLD STATE HOUSE
OLD CORNER BOOKSTORE
BOSTON MASSACRE SITE
PAUL REVERE HOUSE